W9-CGU-263

A NOTE TO PARENTS

Disney's **First Readers Level 2** books were created for beginning readers who are gaining confidence in their early reading skills.

Compared to Level 1 books, **Level 2** books have slightly smaller type and contain more words to a page. Although sentence structure is still simple, the stories are slightly longer and more complex.

Just as children need training wheels when learning to ride a bicycle, they need the support of a good model when learning to read. Every time your child sees that you enjoy reading, whether alone or with him or her, you provide the encouragement needed to build reading confidence. Here are some helpful hints to use with the **Disney's First Readers Level 2** books:

★ Play or act out each character's words. Change your voice to indicate which character is speaking. As your child becomes comfortable with the printed text, he or she can take a favorite character's part and read those passages.

★ Have your child try reading the story. If your child asks about a word, do not interrupt the flow of reading to make him or her sound it out. Pronounce the word for your child. If, however, he or she begins to sound it out, be gently encouraging—your child is developing phonetic skills!

★ Read aloud. It's still important at this level to read to your child. With your child watching, move a finger smoothly along the text. Do not stop at each word. Change the tone of your voice to indicate punctuation marks, such as questions and exclamations. Your child will begin to notice how words and punctuation marks make sense and can make reading fun.

★ Let your child ask you questions about the story. This will help to develop your child's critical thinking skills. Use the After-Reading Fun activities provided at the end of each book as a fun exercise to further enhance your child's reading skills.

★ Praise all reading efforts warmly and often!

Remember that early-reading experiences that you share with your child can help him or her to become a confident and successful reader later on!

— Patricia Koppman
Past President
International Reading Association

For Jonathan, Jason, and Ryan

Pencils by Scott Tilley and Denise Shimabukoro

Copyright © 1998 by Disney Enterprises, Inc./Pixar Animation Studios.
All rights reserved.

No part of this publication may be reproduced in whole or in part,
or stored in a retrieval system, or transmitted in any form or by any means,
electronic, mechanical, photocopying, recording, or otherwise,
without written permission of the copyright holder.
For information regarding permission, write to:
Disney Licensed Publishing,
114 Fifth Avenue, New York, New York 10011

First published by Disney Press, New York, New York.
This edition published by Scholastic Inc.,
90 Old Sherman Turnpike, Danbury, Connecticut 06816
by arrangement with Disney Licensed Publishing.

SCHOLASTIC and associated logos are trademarks of Scholastic Inc.

ISBN 0-7172-8883-8

Printed in the U.S.A.

Flik's Perfect Gift

by Judy Katschke

Disney's First Readers — Level 2
A Story from Disney/Pixar's *A Bug's Life*

SCHOLASTIC INC.

New York   Toronto   London   Auckland   Sydney
Mexico City   New Delhi   Hong Kong   Buenos Aires

It is Queen Atta's birthday.
All the ants are bringing gifts!

But what's bugging Flik?
"I want to bring the *perfect*
gift!" Flik says.

Flik looks high. Flik looks low.
Finding the perfect gift is
no picnic!

Flik thinks and thinks.
"I've got it!" he cries.

Flik's ideas start to bloom!

"It's just a plain old daisy now,"
Flik says. "But soon it will be…"

"A merry-go-round for Atta! Come on, Dot, let's try it out!"

WHOOPS!

"Maybe Atta can use a nice, cool breeze!" Flik says.

"Get ready to chill, Dot!"

WHOOSH!

"Or how about a new way for Atta to fly?" Flik says.

"Hop on, Dot!"

"Maybe you should just get Atta
a card," Dot says.
"I will not give up," Flik cries.
"I *will* find the perfect present!"

"I'll build her a beach umbrella!"
Flik says. "A sprinkler! A ferris wheel!"

Uh-oh. It's Queen Atta!

"What's that, Flik?"
Queen Atta asks.

"It's just a plain old daisy," Flik says.
"It's *perfect*," Queen Atta cries.

"It is?" Flik asks. He looks at the daisy and smiles. "It *is!* Happy birthday, Atta!"

Enhance the reading experience with follow-up questions to help your child develop reading comprehension and increase his/her awareness of words.

Approach this with a sense of play. Make a game of having your child answer the questions. You do not need to ask all the questions at one time. Let these questions be fun discussions rather than a test. If your child doesn't have instant recall, encourage him/her to look back into the book to "research" the answers. You'll be modeling what good readers do and, at the same time, forging a sharing bond with your child.

Flik's Perfect Gift

1a. What are the three things Flik tries to make out of the daisy?

1b. What do the three things have in common?

2. What gift does Dot suggest?

3. Why doesn't Flik want to give the daisy as a gift?

4. What does Flik mean when he says, "Finding the perfect gift is no picnic"?

5. What two words do these contractions stand for: what's, I've, it's, let's, I'll?

Answers: 1a. a merry-go-round, a fan, a flying machine. 1b. they are all things that spin around. 2. a card. 3. he didn't think it was special enough—he thought it was too plain. 5. *possible answer:* it's not easy to find the right gift. 6. what's—what is, I've—I have, it's—it is, let's—let us, I'll—I will.